WILLIAM SHAKESPEARE'S

ROMEO & JULIET

Retold by **Michael Cox**

Illustrated by Steve May

A & C Black • London

Reprinted 2009
First published 2007 by
A & C Black Publishers Ltd
36 Soho Square, London, W1D 3QY

www.acblack.com

Text copyright © 2007 Michael Cox
Illustrations copyright © 2007 Steve May

The rights of Michael Cox and Steve May to be
identified as author and illustrator of this work respectively
have been asserted by them in accordance with the
Copyrights, Designs and Patents Act 1988.

ISBN 978-0-7136-8136-9

A CIP catalogue for this book is available from the British Library.

This book is produced using paper that is made from wood grown
in managed, sustainable forests. It is natural, renewable and
recyclable. The logging and manufacturing processes conform
to the environmental regulations of the country of origin.

Printed and bound in Great Britain
by CPI Cox & Wyman, Reading, RG1 8EX.

Contents

List of characters

Boss Capulet, *head of the Capulet gang*
Lady Capulet, *his wife*
Juliet, *his beautiful daughter*
Tyrone (Tybalt), *his nephew*
Ange, *Juliet's nurse*
Sam (Sampson), *a Capulet gang member*
Greg (Gregory), *a Capulet gang member*
Pete (Peter), *Boss Capulet's errand boy*
Boss Montague, *head of the Montague gang*
Ma Montague, *his wife*
Romeo, *his handsome son*
Benny (Benvolio), *his nephew*
Baz (Balthasar), *Romeo's 'helper'*
Mark (Mercutio), *a Montague gang member*
Abe (Abraham), *a Montague gang member*
The Big E (Prince Escalus), *Nottingham's number one gangster*
Paris, *his nephew*
Larry (Friar Laurence), *local priest and youth worker*
John (Friar John), *his assistant*

Act One
The Big Fight

It all began down at the shopping precinct last Sunday morning. Me and my mate Abe were hanging around outside Blockbuster, bored out of our brains, kicking an empty Pepsi can around, when up walks two lads called Sam and Greg.

Well, this Sam and Greg are Capulet crew lads. And me and Abe are Montague boys. So there's tension. Especially as we can hear Sam saying how he can take on anyone from the Montague gang, no problem.

Then, just as they're passing Blockbuster, Sam goes to flick his teeth at us. In other words, he wants to show us some serious disrespect, but he chickens out, last minute. Probably because Abe has just given him the 'look' and said, 'You want to start something, or what?'

So, having thought twice about the tooth-flicking, Sam ends up with his thumb stuck halfway in his gob, looking like he's missing his dummy! After that, the four of us just stand there, with no one quite ready to make the first move. But not for long. For at that moment, who should come out of Blockbuster, but Tyrone!

Now, this Tyrone is another one of the Capulet crew. But he's older than us. A sort of underboss in charge of the younger gang members. And he's one mean dude.

Straightaway, Tyrone can see there's an atmosphere between his boys and us. So Sam and Greg are on the spot. They know they can't back down now or they'll look like wimps. They've got to do something. And that's when the fight starts!

But listen, I'm getting ahead of myself. Before I tell you about the fight and all the shocking, gruesome stuff that followed it, I'd better introduce myself. My name's Barry. But you can call me Baz. All my mates do.

As you've probably worked out, it's a bit rough round our way. Nicking cars, mugging and stuff goes on nearly all the time. There's even a few drive-by shootings. But mainly at weekends and holidays. A lot of people reckon ours is the roughest estate in Nottingham.

And that's saying something!

The two most powerful families on the estate are the Montagues and the Capulets. They're up to all sorts: car-jacking; credit-card scams, burglary and anything else you can think of. If ever there's a mugging or a drive-by, the cops are round their places like a shot. Montagues and Capulets collect ASBOs like other families collect Tesco loyalty points. What's more, they hate each other's guts.

If you want to survive on our estate you've got to be loyal to one family or the other. Me and Abe are Montague boys. Mainly because we've been mates with Boss Montague's son, Romeo, ever since we were all at infants together. Over the years, I've become Romeo's helper, running his messages, making deliveries for him, keeping him up to speed about the word on the street, that sort of thing. And it's Romeo this story's about. Plus the beautiful Juliet. But we'll come to her in a bit.

So, as I was saying, what with the drive-bys and the robberies and the muggings, there's never a dull moment. And last week it was extremely lively. I mean, one gang fight, three murders and two suicides on one council estate in a single week is a lot in anyone's book.

And after all the crazy, weird stuff that went on, there's been TV vans and reporters all over the place, going up to everyone and trying to get them to talk about it.

Then there were all the cops and forensic teams and detectives who swarmed down here, knocking on doors, pulling people in for questioning and searching around for evidence so they could get to the bottom of it all. Not that they ever will.

To be honest, you're never going to discover how all these things happened by watching it on TV or reading about it in the papers. Why? Because people round our way don't ever tell the truth to reporters or cops. Especially cops.

If you want to know what *really* went on, then I'm the lad to tell you. Because I've been in on the whole thing from the word go. So, listen up and get ready to hear the facts behind the whole amazing story. And first, let's go back to the fight down at the shopping precinct last Sunday morning...

Now, as soon as Tyrone shows up, Greg starts pushing my mate Abe and saying, 'What you looking at, lard-boy? You Montague moron!'

At which point, Sam realises that if he wants to look good, he has to get into the action, too. So he grabs hold of my shirt and says, 'Want some then, do you?'

Now, that's the sort of thing you can't just walk away from. Because if you do, the whole estate will hear about it and your reputation will be zero! So I gave Sam one of my sweetest, friendliest smiles. Then I nutted him. And, before you can yell 'Fight!' the four of us are rolling around on the pavement scuffling, punching and cursing! Then, suddenly, we heard a screech of tyres and this red Golf GTi with blacked-out windows pulls up at the kerb right next to us.

It's Benny, who's one of our lot. He tries to calm us all down, but just as he's trying to pull Sam and me apart, Tyrone grabs hold of him and says, 'Leave it, you Montague fudge-sucker!'

So Benny smacks him in the mouth and it all starts to get extremely physical. Then, what with the shouting and the sound of breaking glass (btw: that's Sam going through Blockbuster's front window), it seems like every lad off our estate has suddenly turned up.

What a scrap! There must have been about 80 of us going at it.

And then it gets even worse. This black Porsche swerves into one end of the car park, while a silver S-class Mercedes roars into the other. Out of the Porsche jumps Boss Montague, wearing enough brass knuckles to keep our local dentist busy for months, while

Boss Capulet leaps out of the Merc, swinging his own weapon of choice – a battle-scarred baseball bat he calls the Nutcracker. They look like they're going to kill each other. But what stops them is the sound of a single gunshot echoing around the precinct. In fact, it stops us all.

We look round to see a figure standing outside the betting shop. The sun's glinting off his shiny, shaved head and he's wearing this white tracksuit and gold trainers, plus a silver T-shirt with a big Hugo Boss logo on the front. Even though half his face is hidden behind his Ray Bans, we can tell that he's very, very angry. His four minders aren't looking too happy, either.

Now, Prince Escalus, or the Big E as most people call him, is the biggest noise on the whole estate. Even the Capulets and the Montagues are scared of him. In the past, he's had some very bad things done to people who've upset him. And he's got connections all over the place.

15

'You bunch of losers!' he roars. 'On pain of torture, from those bloody hands, throw your weapons to the ground. Can't you hear that?'

We listen. It's the sound of cop cars.

Now, the Big E owns betting shops, nightclubs and stuff all over Nottingham. And he's well in with the local cops, who usually turn a blind eye to all his dodgy little 'deals'. So the last thing he wants is to cause his 'pals' any problems.

'*Now*!' he shouts. 'And if any of you lot are still here after I've counted to five, I just hope you've paid your medical insurance!'

In five seconds the precinct's empty! So that's that, we all think. End of story. But in fact, it's just the beginning...

About ten minutes after the fight, Benny's talking to Romeo's dad.

'Where's our Romeo got to, Benny?' Boss Montague asks.

'Dunno,' says Benny. 'I haven't seen him since this morning. He was wandering round

16

the park before it got light. Talking to himself.'

'Something must be on his mind,' mutters Boss Montague. 'Look! Talk of the devil! Here he comes now! Right, find out what's troubling him, Benny.'

'Trust me, boss!' whispers Benny.

Then, before Romeo sees him, Boss Montague leaves.

'Benny!' says Romeo, looking all moody.

'What's up, man?' says Benny. 'Why the long face?'

'Woman trouble,' mumbles Romeo. 'It's doing my head in.'

'Forget it!' says Benny. 'This place is full of tasty babes. And with your film-star looks, you can have your pick of them. Anyway, who is she?'

'That's for me to know and you to find out,' says Romeo.

At this moment, who should come up, but Pete. Pete was in juniors with us, now he's an errand boy for the Capulets. He's a bit slow, but harmless enough. Anyway, he's peering at a piece of paper, looking really puzzled.

'What's up, Pete?' says Benny.

'Oh, hi, Benny,' says Pete. 'There's gonna be this big party up at the Capulets' place tomorrow night. Something to do with them suckin' up to the Big E. Boss Capulet has given me this list of all the people who're coming. He's told me to go round and invite them all personally.' Then he goes really red and says, 'But I've broke me specs, so I can't read it.'

'You clown!' laughs Benny. 'Broke your specs! You can't read! Everyone knows that!'

'Give it here, Pete,' says Romeo and he looks at the list. All of a sudden, he brightens up. 'Look, Benny! *She's* been invited!'

'Who's she?' says Benny.

'Rose!' laughs Romeo. 'The girl you were trying to find out about.'

'Why don't we crash the party then?' says Benny.

'OK!' says Romeo, with a grin. 'Sounds good to me.'

So, the next evening, Romeo, Benny, and their mate Mark, meet outside Mr Kwok's chip shop in the precinct. Benny and Mark are both looking like they've lost a quid then found a fiver. Probably because they're pretty sure they're gonna be scoring with some really hot girls at the party. But Romeo's not looking too happy.

'Ready then?' says Benny, checking his hair in Mr Kwok's window.

'No, I've changed my mind,' says Romeo.

'What!' yells Benny. 'Why would you do that?'

'I had this weird dream,' says Romeo. 'It sort of warned me that if we go to this party, it'll lead to loads of really bad stuff happening.'

'Rubbish!' laughs Benny. 'Dreams can't tell the future, man!'

'Come on, you aren't backing out now!' says Mark. Then he blows Romeo a kiss, puts his hands on his hips, gives a little wiggle and says, 'Don't forget who's gonna be there!'

Romeo laughs and says, 'All right then! I suppose you've got a point!'

So the three of them crash the party at the Capulets'. Which is a pretty cool place! Boss Capulet's massive Merc is parked out the front with its CAP 1 personalised number plates. Next to it is Ma Capulet's purple Peugeot, with about ten thousand fluffy toy kittens and puppies piled up on the parcel shelf. Nice touch that, even if I do say so.

Inside the house, there's a massive widescreen TV, purple fridge-freezer as big as a wardrobe, gold taps in the downstairs bog, and a huge conservatory out the back. They've even got a fancy balcony!

When the guys walk in, no one recognises them because they're wearing hoodies. Boss Capulet's sitting in a corner, dripping with bling, stroking this massive Alsatian and muttering to a couple of hard-cases with eyes like ferrets and necks like birthday cakes. Both of them are stroking their chins and looking dead shifty. Probably planning a job!

Ma Capulet's wandering around in a purple lurex top, skintight, lilac leather trousers and silver stilettos which are so high it makes you feel dizzy just looking at her. She's fluttering her false eyelashes and grinning like crazy so's everyone can see the brilliant-white paint job she's just had on her teeth! And she's talking in that put-on snobby voice she always uses, because she thinks her family are the poshest on the estate. As if!

The DJ's got RnB blasting out so loud you can hear it five streets away and there's a whole load of kids dancing and yelling at each other as they try to brush up on their lip-reading skills.

Mark and Benny immediately zero in on a couple of girls and get straight into strutting their stuff. But Romeo just leans against the wall, studying his fingernails and looking totally cool, knowing (as usual) that he's the best-looking guy in the place. But then, only about a minute has passed when his stomach knots, his heart booms and his legs turn to jelly. Why? Because he's seen the most stunning babe he's ever laid eyes on in his life. He can't believe how perfect this girl is! If he'd designed her himself he couldn't have come anywhere near the living miracle he's eyeballing right now.

But get this – *it's not Rose*!

Who is she? She's the drop-dead gorgeous Juliet. She's dancing with her mates and, as she does, her lovely eyes sparkle and her long, black hair sways this way and that, making Romeo feel like falling to his knees and proposing to her on the spot. As she smiles her stunning smile and dips and shakes and shimmies to the music, Romeo follows her every move. He can't take his eyes off her. Talk about poetry in motion!

Of course, Romeo doesn't know who this stunning vision is yet. But what he does know is that he's just got to get up close and personal. And fast! But then things get interesting, because standing quite near to Juliet and her mates, chewing gum and looking like he thinks he's the coolest cat in the universe, is this hard-case in an Armani leather jacket. It's Tyrone. And straightaway he recognises Romeo!

'Here, you Montague scumsucker!' he says. 'You've got some nerve turning up here. An' you're soon gonna wish you hadn't!' Then he turns to a mate and whispers.

The guy goes off, but he's back in a flash with a Tesco carrier bag. Everyone knows what's in it. It's Tyrone's blade.

Act Two
Star-crossed Lovers

Just as Tyrone's reaching into the carrier bag, Boss Capulet spots him.

'Leave it, Tyrone!' he says. 'I don't want my party spoiling!'

Now Tyrone gets stroppy and, pointing to Romeo, he says, 'When such a villain is a guest. I'll not endure him!'

'Show me some respect, boy!' snarls Boss Capulet. 'Don't forget who the main man is around here!' Then the Alsatian stands up and snarls, too. Like it's giving him back-up.

So Tyrone walks away. You don't cross people like Boss Capulet. He mutters something about finishing this with Romeo some other time, and splits.

The party starts up again and Romeo wastes no time making his move on Juliet. Before you can say 'Star-crossed lovers!' they're pecking and necking! Yes, it's taken about two minutes for them to go completely nuts about each other.

But then, just as things are really warming up, old Ange, who's looked after Juliet ever since she was little, comes over and yells, 'Jules, yer mam wants yer!'

So they have to cool it.

'Tell me,' Romeo says to Ange, when Juliet has left. 'Who *is* Juliet's mam?'

'Ma Capulet of course!' giggles Ange.

Yes, you've got it! The new love in Romeo Montague's life is Boss Capulet's daughter. Romeo's been smooching with the enemy! It's time to get out of there fast.

Now it's Juliet's turn to get curious. 'Who were those guys, Ange?' she asks.

'Well, I know two were Benny and Mark from the other end of the estate,' says Ange. 'But as for the third, really good-looking one, I've no idea. I'll find out if you like!'

'Yes, do that!' says Juliet.

A few seconds later, Ange is back with the news that the mystery guy is called Romeo Montague. So of course Juliet freaks out!

On the way home, Romeo decides he's just got to see some more of this lovely girl miracle called Juliet. Even if she is a Capulet! So he slips away from his mates, climbs over the Capulets' fence and hides in their back garden. Then he looks up at the balcony. And who should be standing there, but Juliet, talking to herself!

'Oh, Romeo!' she goes. 'Oh, Romeo, Romeo! Wherefore art thou, Romeo?'

'I could call myself something else, if you like, darling!' whispers Romeo from the darkness, giving Juliet such a shock that she almost falls off the balcony!

'What the...?' she gasps. 'Is that you, Romeo?'

'Sure is, babe!' calls Romeo.

'Oh no!' squeals Juliet. 'If my family find you down there, you've had it!'

'Don't care,' says Romeo. 'I'd sooner get wasted than not see you again. I'm mad about you!'

'And I'm mad about *you*,' whispers Juliet.

'Well,' says Romeo. 'There's only one thing for it – we'll have to get married!'

'Yes, Romeo,' murmurs Juliet 'We will, my love.'

'Leave it to me, babe!' calls Romeo. 'I'll sort out everything. Then I'll let you know where and when.'

'All right, darling!' says Juliet. 'I'll send old Ange to get the message in the morning. Love you!'

'Love you, too!' says Romeo. 'Missing you already!'

'Me too!' says Juliet. 'Goodnight, goodnight. Parting is such sweet sorrow.'

So Romeo legs it. And starts planning how to fix their wedding. Sounds crazy, but that's what love does to people. Not that I'd know.

Next day, Romeo calls on this guy called Larry. He runs the local youth club and is the official do-gooder on our estate. I think he might be a vicar, cos sometimes he does weddings and funerals, too. But he doesn't wear weird frocks. He's a really decent bloke. If you've got a problem, you can talk to

Larry. Which is good, cos round here you can't tell your troubles to your mates. They just call you a wimp.

When Romeo shows up, Larry's in his garden, picking carrots.

'Hi, Romeo!' he says. 'You look like you've been up all night.'

'I have, Larry,' says Romeo.

'Were you with Rose?' says Larry, with a grin. 'You naughty boy!'

'No, not her,' says Romeo. 'I've gone completely nuts over someone else now. She's called Juliet.'

'Juliet who?' asks Larry.

'Capulet,' replies Romeo with a grin.

'You're joking!' gasps Larry, dropping his carrots.

'It's true,' says Romeo. 'She loves me and I love her and that's that! And I want you to marry us. But on the quiet. Can you do that?'

'I can,' says Larry. 'But yesterday you were nuts about Rose!'

'This time it's for real, Larry,' says Romeo.

31

'Me and Juliet are desperate. Please say you'll do it.'

Larry thinks for a minute then says, 'All right, I will. You never know, if you two get married, it might bring those fighting families of yours together!'

'Brilliant!' cries Romeo. 'Let's get busy then.'

'We will, Romeo,' says Larry. 'But remember – wisely and slow; they stumble that run fast.'

Next morning, Benny and Mark meet up outside Mr Kwok's.

'You seen Romeo anywhere?' says Mark.

'Na!' says Benny. 'He's probably still swooning over that Rose bird. But here's news for you. Tyrone's going round saying he's gonna do Romeo. Give him a right slappin'. Or worse!'

Then who should turn up but Romeo. He was coming across the wasteground.

'Hey, Benny,' says Mark. 'Look what the cat's dragged in!'

'Romeo! Where did you get to last night, lover-boy?' Benny laughs.

'Bit of business,' says Romeo, with a grin. 'Had something to sort out.'

But before he can say any more, old Ange arrives.

'Ange!' says Mark. 'You're looking right tasty today, darlin'!'

'More than I can say for you, gorilla-gob!' snaps Ange. 'Anyway, I wanna private word with Romeo. So why don't you two go and play with the traffic!'

'OK, babe!' says Mark, giving Ange a playful wink. 'But I'll be back. I can't get enough of you, darlin'!'

'Cheeky devil!' says Ange, as Mark and Benny split. Then she turns to Romeo and says, 'Right, what's this message I got to give to Jules?'

'Tell her it's all sorted,' says Romeo. 'She's to meet me at Larry's place this afternoon. You come with her and wait at the back of the youth club. One of my mates will bring you a rope ladder. Make sure it's hanging from Juliet's balcony tonight! Got that?'

'No probs!' says Ange.

'Cool!' says Romeo. 'And here's a fiver for your trouble!'

'Nice one!' says Ange, as she pockets the cash.

So old Ange goes back to Juliet and tells her the set up. And, before you can say 'Mr and Mrs Montague', Romeo and Juliet are over at Larry's place and he's married them, all lawful and legal! Of course, they're both over the moon and can't wait to spend some 'quality' time together, once Ange has done her stuff with the ladder later that night.

But, life being what it is, what they don't know is that Romeo is about to get himself in some very serious bother. Bother that will lead to all sorts of nasty complications. Not to mention a really busy week for our local undertaker.

Act Three
You're a
Dead Man!

This is how it all starts to unravel. Benny and Mark are hanging out at the precinct. It's dead hot and flies are buzzing round the KFC family buckets and MacDonalds wrappers that have been dumped in the broken fountain. Snotty little kids in their underwear are milling around the ice-cream van, clutching their fifty pence pieces, elbowing and pushing each other so they can be first to get served. A couple of them have already started to scrap, shoving and punching each other and using some very grown-up swear words. But their mums don't give a monkey's. They're all standing outside Mr Kwoks, sharing fags and comparing their tattoos. Which is almost all they're wearing today.

'I've heard the Capulet lads are coming here later on,' Benny says to Mark. 'Do you reckon there's gonna be trouble?'

'We can handle it, can't we?' replies Mark. He glances at the two little kids, who're now rolling around on the ground, grunting and groaning, as they try to beat the daylights out of each other. He jerks his thumb towards them, then he laughs and says, 'I mean, you're up for a scrap, aren't you, Benny?'

'Yeah, I suppose so,' says Benny. But his eyes are saying something different from his mouth.

Trying to boost him up a bit, Mark says, 'I know you been in some scraps in your time, Benny. An' done pretty good, I hear!'

'Yeah, s'pose I have!' laughs Benny. But he's still looking like he wishes he was somewhere else.

Then, all of a sudden, three lads walk round the corner. They're wearing the black baggies, ice-blue T-shirts and red-spotted bandannas the Capulet crew favour. And they're heading straight for Mark and Benny.

'Look who's here, Mark!' says Benny. 'It's Tyrone an' his crew!'

'Let them!' says Mark. 'If there's gonna be a scrap, I know who's gonna end up gettin' a kickin'. And it's not gonna be me or you!'

'Hey, you!' says Tyrone, going up to Mark and putting his face so close that Mark can smell his Lynx and fag smoke and see the forest of blackheads on his big, lumpy nose. 'I wanna word with you!'

'Just a word?' says Mark. 'Or something else? Like a scrap?'

'Not with you!' says Tyrone. 'It's Romeo I want to get physical with. Me and him have unfinished business. But you're his mate, aren't you?'

'Yeah, I am!' says Mark. 'An' if anyone wants trouble with him, they got trouble with me, too! So, do you wanna do something about it, pizza-face?' Then, quick as a flash, Mark sticks his hand in his pocket, pulls out this dirty great knife, waves it in front of Tyrone's face and says, 'Come on, you Capulet scumball! Want some, do you?'

'Cool it, lads,' says Benny. 'There's too many people watching!'

'So what!' says Mark, who's really up for it now. 'That's what they've got eyes for.'

But then, just as it seems like a scrap is going to start, Romeo turns up.

'Ah! Just the guy I'm looking for!' says Tyrone, turning his back on Mark. Then he goes up to Romeo and says, 'What were you thinkin' of last night? Gatecrashin' my uncle's private party like that. That was seriously disrespectful. An' now you got me to answer to!'

But the thing is, even though Tyrone's winding him up something rotten, Romeo doesn't get angry. Why? Because he's just married Juliet! And she's Tyrone's cousin. Romeo's probably even thinking something like this guy's 'family' now and the last thing I wanna do is start scrapping with the wife's rellies!

Mark can't believe what he's seeing. Romeo's starting to look like the biggest wimp on the estate. 'Come on, Romeo!' he yells. 'You can't let this scumbag talk to you like that. You gotta do something. You losin' your nerve or what?' Then he says to Tyrone,

'You're pushing your luck, you are! I'm gonna wipe the floor with you!'

'Look, you two, cool it!' says Romeo. 'You heard what the Big E said would happen if there's any more trouble.'

But he might as well be talking to the empty chip bag next to his foot.

'Leave off, dog's breath!' says Tyrone, pushing Mark away.

'Why should I?' says Mark, shoving Tyrone really hard.

That's enough for Tyrone. His eyes go narrow and his mouth goes all small and tight. Quick as a flash, he pulls his knife and goes for Mark's throat. But Mark's too quick for him. He sidesteps Tyrone then dances towards him, holding his own blade out, looking for a chance to do some serious damage.

By now, the two little kids have stopped scrapping and are standing side-by-side, all sweaty and snotty, staring at Mark and Tyrone with their gobs wide open.

Realising there's gonna be trouble, all the mums now start grabbing hold of their kids and giving each other knowing looks. But they don't make any attempt to leave. Why? Because they don't want to miss a good scrap, do they?

'Benny!' yells Romeo. 'We've gotta stop this. Help me split them up!'

But Benny just stands there. So Romeo realises it's up to him. He grabs Mark's knife-hand and tries to push him away. Which gives Tyrone the chance he's looking for. Quick as lightning, he rams his knife into Mark. Right between the ribs!

As the mums and kids begin to scream, Mark makes this 'Hmmph!' noise and his eyes suddenly go big, as if they're gonna pop out of his head. Then he stares down at the blood on his shirt like he can't believe what he's seeing.

Tyrone pulls back, wipes his knife on his sleeve, then turns to his mates. 'Leg it, lads!' he shouts.

At first, Romeo and Benny think everything's OK, cos there isn't much blood.

'Mark?' says Benny. 'Are you hurt, mate?'

'Na! S'just a scratch,' says Mark. Then he starts coughing up blood and says, 'Course I'm hurt, you dingbat! I've just been stabbed!'

'Don't worry!' says Romeo. 'It's probably not too bad.'

'Yes, it is,' says Mark, as more blood dribbles out the side of his mouth. 'I'm done for. And it's all your fault!'

'I was only tryin' to help,' says Romeo.

'I feel dead weird,' gasps Mark, turning to Benny. 'I need to sit down. Help us over to the chippy, mate!'

So Benny puts his arm round him and helps Mark over to Mr Kwok's. As they go, Mark looks over his shoulder and says, 'You're nothing but trouble, Romeo! An' all the other Montagues an' Capulets! A curse on both your houses!'

Benny's soon back. He's covered in blood and looks like he's in some sort of nightmare.

'He's dead, mate!' he says. 'Mark's dead!'

'You're kidding!' says Romeo quietly. He shakes his head. 'I reckon this is only just the beginning!'

And he's right. It's not long before Tyrone comes back! As soon as Romeo sees him, he runs over and grabs hold of his throat. 'You murdering sleazeball!' he yells. 'You've just killed my mate! Now you're going where he's gone!' Then he pulls his knife.

So Tyrone pulls his blade, too.

Now, Tyrone's a good streetfighter. But Romeo's really angry. They've only been weaving and dodging a few minutes when Tyrone suddenly screams and backs away. He falls to the ground. And the next moment, there's another stiff on the pavement.

'Romeo!' gasps Benny. 'You've killed Tyrone! You'd better split!'

But Romeo just stands there, looking down at Tyrone's body.

'Leg it, Romeo, you dimwit!' Benny screams, and Romeo finally runs off.

Next second, the whole precinct's full of people pushing and shouting and trying to get a look at Tyrone's body. The Big E shoves his way through the crowd, followed by Boss Montague, Boss Capulet and their wives.

'Who started it, Benny?' says the Big E.

'I can explain everything,' says Benny. 'Tyrone did Mark, so Romeo did Tyrone!'

Ma Capulet goes crazy, 'That's my brother's boy lying there, Big E!' she yells. 'A Montague must pay for this!'

The Big E ignores her and says, 'Answer my question, Benny! Who started it?'

'It was Tyrone,' says Benny. 'He was winding Romeo up something rotten.'

'Take no notice of him, Big E!' shouts Ma Capulet. 'He would say that. He's Romeo's friend! You've got to kill Romeo!'

'No, you can't do that!' says Boss Montague. 'Our kid only did Tyrone cos he did his mate. And that's fair and proper!'

The Big E thinks for a minute, then says, 'I want Romeo off this estate and out of

Nottingham for good. He's got one hour. If I find out he's still around after that, he's a dead man.'

That evening, knowing nothing about the stuff that's gone on down at the precinct, Juliet is in her bedroom. It's got glittery pink walls and a really thick, lilac carpet, the sort that your feet sink right into and make nice shadow patterns when you walk across it. And she's got one of those really cool, four-poster beds, with curtains you can pull shut to make yourself feel all safe and cosy.

Juliet's feeling anxious. She's flicking through a pile of her mum's old *Hello* and *OK!* magazines while listening to a CD and half watching a soap on her portable TV with the sound turned down.

Some of the time she's going over to her dressing table and checking out her lipstick and eye shadow and stuff. When she's not doing that, she's nipping into her walk-in wardrobe and changing her top every three minutes. But most of all she's wishing it would get dark so she can get it together with Romeo. And then, just as Juliet sighs and chucks yet another copy of *OK!* into the bin, Ange barges in, all out of breath.

'What's the matter?' says Juliet. 'You look awful. Has something bad happened?'

'Really, *really* bad!' gasps Ange. 'He's dead!'

Juliet goes white as a sheet and says, 'Who? My Romeo?'

'I seen his body up the precinct!' groans Ange. 'It were all bloody an' 'orrible! With this dirty great stab wound!'

'Who are you talking about?' screams Juliet, grabbing Ange by the shoulders and shaking her so's her false teeth rattle. 'Is it Romeo?'

'No!' cries Ange. 'It's your cousin, Tyrone. Him and Romeo had a scrap, and Romeo killed Tyrone with his knife. Then he did a runner. And now the Big E says he'll have Romeo killed if he ever shows up in Nottingham again!'

47

'Oh no!' screams Juliet. 'What an idiot! Why did Romeo have to go and do a dumb thing like killing my cousin?' Then she starts blubbing, 'Oh, Ange! I'll never see my lovely Romeo again! I'll never see him again!'

'Well, I could have warned you,' says Ange, with a shrug. 'If you ask me, lads are all as bad as each other. They act first and think second. What I say is, don't expect too much and you won't get disappointed. Anyway, there's plenty more where he came from. He was a waste of space.'

But Juliet isn't having any of that! 'Don't says those things about Romeo!' she shouts. 'I love him. But I'll never see him again! I'll never see him again!'

Which is when Ange says, 'Listen! Romeo's not even left the estate yet. He's hiding.'

'Well, why didn't you tell me?' sobs Juliet.

'I just have!' says Ange. She gives Juliet a big hug. 'And don't worry. I'll go and see him and make sure he comes to you tonight!'

'You're a treasure!' sobs Juliet. She gives

Ange her ring and says, 'O, find him! Give this ring to my true knight. And bid him come to take his last farewell!'

Meanwhile, Romeo's in a right panic. He knows he can't go home, cos the Big E's lads will find him. The only place he can think of going to is Larry's.

So he does.

'I'm in trouble!' gasps Romeo, when Larry opens the door. 'Can you help me out?'

'Of course I can!' says Larry, who's got a real soft spot for Romeo and knows that Tyrone can be a vicious scumball. 'Come on in. You look like you could do with a rest!'

After Romeo's told him his side of things, Larry says, 'Don't worry. You can hide in my basement. There are drinks and food down there. Make yourself at home. I'm going to find out exactly what people are saying.'

About half an hour later, Larry is back.

'Well?' says Romeo, looking really worried. 'What's happening?'

'Well, I suppose it could be worse,' replies Larry. 'The Big E has said you must get out of Nottingham now. For good! But if you ever come back, him and his heavies are going to kill you!'

Romeo takes this real bad. 'So I'll never see Juliet again. But I can't live without her, Larry. I can't!'

'Look, Romeo!' says Larry. 'Consider yourself lucky. You've still got Juliet and you're both alive. And where there's life, there's hope.'

Just then, there's a knock on the door and Larry almost jumps out of his skin. 'Quickly!' he says. 'Get back to the basement. It could be the Big E. Or some of the Capulets come to murder you themselves!'

'Let them!' groans Romeo.

'Who's there?' shouts Larry.

'I got a message for Romeo,' says a voice. 'From Juliet. It's Ange!'

So Larry lets her in. 'You had me worried there,' he says.

'Where's Romeo?' says Ange. Then she spots him, sulking in the corner. 'I've just come from the Capulets',' she says. 'Juliet's just as cut up about what's happened as you are. Why don't you act like a man, rather than a big kid?'

Romeo looks up at Ange and says, 'But doesn't she hate my guts for killing her cousin?'

'Course not!' says Ange. 'She's mad about you. And she sent you this to prove it.' Then she gives Romeo Juliet's ring and says, 'So quit sulking!'

'Yes, stop feeling sorry for yourself,' says Larry. 'And listen, I think you should still stick to the plan of going to see her tonight.'

'And so do I!' says Ange, giving Romeo a wink.

'You do?' says Romeo, suddenly loads happier.

'Yes!' says Larry. He turns to Ange. 'You go back to Juliet now. Tell her that Romeo will be there soon!'

The moment Ange is out the door, Larry turns to Romeo and says, 'I've got another idea, too.'

'Tell me about it!' says Romeo.

'Well,' says Larry. 'I've got the keys to a flat in Manchester. It's my brother's, but he's off in Africa doing work with Oxfam. So it's yours, if you want it. You can lie low there for a while. Until things have calmed down.'

'Sounds good to me,' says Romeo.

'And in the meantime,' says Larry. 'Let's hope the Big E finds out the truth about the Tyrone thing and decides to let you off. Then you can come back and announce your marriage to Juliet. You never know, it might even take some of the heat out of the situation between your two families.'

'Yeah, that sounds more like it,' says Romeo, grinning from ear to ear. 'I knew you'd come up with something, Larry. Thanks, mate!'

'Now listen,' continues Larry. 'After you've been to see Juliet tonight, you must leave

Nottingham, and fast!' He reaches into his pocket and hands Romeo a key and slip of paper. 'Here's the key and address for the flat. Make yourself cosy up there. But, whatever you do, don't use the phone or email. Or your mobile or credit cards. The Big E's got the police in his pocket. They'll be tracking you by your calls and credit-card transactions. And the Big E knows that we're friends. So they'll definitely have a bug on my phones, too! If I need to get a message to you, I'll send it with my mate, John.'

Larry reaches into his pocket again and takes out a wad of cash, which he shoves into Romeo's hand, saying, 'Here's some money for petrol and food.'

'Thanks!' says Romeo. Then he starts counting the seconds till dark.

Act Four
You Couldn't
Make it Up

Now, get this! While all this other stuff's going on, Boss Capulet really puts the Rottweiler among the kittens – by going and telling the Big E's nephew, Paris, that he can marry Juliet! It's a sort of business arrangement for the old guy. If he can get his Juliet hitched to the nephew of the biggest noise on our estate, it means he'll be well in there and that favours can be asked. Which, of course, will give him the edge over the Montagues.

Paris is over the moon about all this because he fancies Juliet something rotten (and who can blame him?). Now, Boss Capulet is dead keen to get the wedding all done and dusted. So he decides to have it sooner rather than later and sets the date for the coming Thursday! Which is gonna make things a bit awkward for Romeo and Juliet!

Not that they're bothered right now. Why? Because the moment it's got dark, Romeo's up the rope ladder like a squirrel up a nut tree. And (to put it politely) he and Juliet are tucked up all nice and cosy in that massive four-poster of hers. Its thick, pink-velvet curtains have been pulled tight for hours now. Yes! Romeo and Juliet have been dancing the bedspring boogy the whole night long! All just metres above Ma and Boss Capulets' heads, who are downstairs in the lounge, rabbiting on about who to invite to the wedding and whether to have a sit-down meal or a buffet.

I mean, how weird is that? You couldn't make it up, could you?

When it gets light, no way does Juliet want Romeo to go.

'Please stay a bit longer,' she says, stroking Romeo's hair. 'It isn't properly morning yet.'

'All right,' says Romeo. 'But we're pushing our luck.'

The next minute, they're interrupted by Ange sticking her head round the bedroom door.

'Yer mam's coming!' she whispers.

'Quick, Romeo!' squeals Juliet. 'You must leave – now!'

Romeo's out of there like a shot, still pulling on his socks as he staggers over to the balcony and clambers down the rope ladder to the garden.

'Stay in touch, my darling!' calls Juliet from the balcony. 'Every minute's going to seem like a day with you gone!' She starts sobbing, 'Oh, Romeo, do you think we will ever see each other again?'

'Course we will!' says Romeo. 'We'll be together in no time!'

'But just looking down at you now makes me feel all spooky,' says Juliet. 'Like I'm seeing you dead in a coffin!'

'That's just cos I'm a bit pale and tired with being up all night. You look just the same, babe!' says Romeo. Then he glances around and says, 'OK! I'm gonna split. See you soon!' He blows her a kiss, then legs it. As he lets himself out the back gate, Juliet blows him a kiss, too. Then she bursts into tears.

'Oh, you poor girl!' says her mam, as she comes in and sees Juliet blubbing. 'You're still upset about Tyrone's murder, aren't you?'

Juliet sort of sniffs and nods and looks dead pathetic.

'And I sympathise with you, my dear!' says Ma Capulet, stroking Juliet's long, black hair. 'Just knowing that dreadful Romeo Montague is still walking around free and alive really makes my blood boil! But don't worry, your father and I have contacts. Soon, one of them will pay Romeo a visit. Maybe they'll sit next to him in a pub and slip something into his drink. Something to end his worthless life!'

'Yes, and if you gave it to me first, I could add something to it, too!' says Juliet, meaning she would dilute it, so it wouldn't kill him.

Her mam nods and says, 'Now, stop your crying! I've got some great news for you. News that will really cheer you!'

'What?' says Juliet.

'Your father's given his permission for Paris

to marry you!' squeals her mam, clapping her hands together so hard that she almost snaps off her massive purple nail extensions. 'Isn't that simply wonderful news, my dear?'

Juliet drops back down on the bed with a bump. She is totally gobsmacked. She can hardly believe her ears. 'When?' she blurts out.

'This Thursday!' squeals Ma Capulet.

'But we hardly know each other,' says Juliet, still wondering if this is for real. 'I don't even find him attractive!' Then she takes a deep breath and says, 'Look, Mum! Tell Dad I'm not doing it. I'd sooner marry Romeo Montague. And you know how much I hate him!'

Which is when Boss Capulet walks in.

'Well, here's your father now!' says Ma Capulet. 'You'd better tell him what you've just told me!'

'Still crying over Tyrone, love?' says Boss Capulet. Then he turns to his wife and says, 'I thought she'd be happy. Now she knows she's gonna marry Paris.'

'She says she doesn't want to marry Paris!' says Ma Capulet.

'WHAT!' yells Boss Capulet. 'YOU'RE JOKING!'

But one look at Juliet is enough to tell him she isn't.

'I'm not going to marry him, Dad!' she sniffs.

'YES, YOU BLINKING WELL ARE!' roars her dad. He looks round at everyone. 'I can't believe this! She doesn't know how lucky she is. When I think of all the trouble I've gone to, to set this wedding up. An' what a catch! That Paris is minted! Massive 4x4! New jet ski! Top-of-the-range sunbed! His bling is probably worth more than most people round here could make in five years! What more could a girl want? She ought to be pleased to bits!'

'*Pleased?*' screams Juliet. 'You're joking! I hate the thought of marrying that creepy slime bag with his orange skin and stinky armpits!'

'Well,' growls her dad, getting that really mean look he gets when he's gonna have his own way, no matter what. 'You ain't got no choice, darlin'! You're gonna marry him. An' that's that!'

'But, Dad...' sobs Juliet.

'Shut up!' he roars. 'Or you'll feel the back of my 'and! You're marrying him, you ungrateful little brat! End of story!' Then he storms out, slamming the door so hard it almost jumps off its hinges.

Juliet turns to her mam. 'I'd sooner be dead than marry Paris!' she pleads.

'That's as may be, young lady!' says her mam, all hoity-toity. 'But you heard what your father just said!' Then she goes out, too.

Now Juliet turns to Ange, but she just says, 'You'd better do as your dad says, love. I mean, that Paris is well loaded, what with his uncle being the Big E. And if yer 'onest, ducks, your Romeo's a dead man!'

Juliet is gutted! There's only one thing for it. She decides to go to Larry and see if he can help. Failing that, she thinks, she can always top herself.

That Tuesday, all excited about the idea of getting it on with Juliet, Paris goes round to Larry's to sort out the wedding.

Larry's in his front garden, pruning roses, when Paris turns up. And he's totally gobsmacked when he hears the news. But he decides the best way to handle things is to stay cool and think fast.

'All ready for the big day, then?' he says. 'I suppose you've had a nice cosy chat with Juliet about the honeymoon and everything!'

Paris coughs, looks a bit sheepish, then says, 'Well, we haven't had much chance to get together really. What with her being so upset about Tyrone. She's sort of kept a bit distant from me, if you know what I mean.'

At this moment, Juliet turns up at the gate.

Paris gives her a big smile and says, 'Hi, babe, my drop-dead-gorgeous darling!' Then he adds, 'Or should I be calling you my gorgeous little wife!'

'Steady on!' replies Juliet.

Paris ignores this and says, 'You been crying again?'

'That's my business,' snaps Juliet. 'Now listen, I want to have a word with Larry. Alone. So just leave us, will you?'

'OK! I know when I'm not wanted,' says Paris, and walks off, whistling like he hasn't a care in the world.

'What a slimeball!' says Juliet, as they go inside. Then she takes a deep breath. 'Look, Larry, I'm not going to marry that creep on Thursday. I'd sooner do away with myself. I'm serious!'

Larry looks worried. 'There's no need to do anything drastic,' he says. 'Listen, I've got an idea that may be the answer to your problems.'

'Great!' says Juliet. 'Tell me about it!'

'OK,' says Larry. 'Though first I should warn you that it's going be uncomfortable.'

'No problem!' says Juliet. 'I'll do anything. Throw myself off the top of the flats.

Get buried alive alongside dead people. Anything you say, Larry.'

'Then listen,' says Larry. 'This is the plan. Just do as I say and everything will work like a dream. First, I want you to go back home and pretend you're really happy. Tell your dad you'll marry Paris.'

At this, Juliet pretends to puke. But then she grins and says, 'Cool! I quite like the idea of doing a bit of acting.'

'That's the spirit!' says Larry, then he slips his hand in his pocket, takes out a small bottle and whispers, 'Right, this is the crucial bit. When you go to bed, make sure Ange isn't hanging around. Then drink this. Don't worry, it won't hurt you. But it will knock you out cold. In fact, if anyone sees you, they'll think you're dead.'

'You're joking!' says Juliet.

'I'm not,' says Larry, with a wink. 'When they come to wake you for the wedding, they'll think you've died and arrange for you to be buried.'

'Gruesome!' groans Juliet. 'But go on, I'm still as keen as ever.'

'Excellent!' says Larry. 'In the meantime, my mate John will be up in Manchester telling Romeo what we're doing. We wouldn't want him accidentally hearing you're dead and doing something silly, would we?'

'Heaven forbid!' gasps Juliet, grabbing hold of Larry's wrist and turning pale. 'Just the thought of it makes me go cold from head to toe.'

'Don't worry!' says Larry. 'It will all go like clockwork. You'll be taken to the undertaker's and laid out in your coffin, then put in the Chapel of Rest, ready for your funeral. You'll be like that for 42 hours and then awake as from a pleasant sleep. The undertaker's a friend of mine. He's agreed to leave the alarm switched off and let Romeo have a key. When you wake up, I'll have Romeo there, ready and waiting.'

'Brilliant, Larry!' says Juliet.

'Thanks,' says Larry, with a blush. 'Then

all it needs is for Romeo to get you out of there, put you on the back of his Kawasaki and head for the M1! Before you know it, you'll both be in Manchester!'

'All set to live happily ever after!' giggles Juliet. 'Thanks for this, Larry. You're a star!'

When Juliet gets home, everyone's busy getting ready for the wedding. Her mum's making sandwiches, her dad's organising the booze and Ange is whizzing round with the hoover.

'Hi, Dad! Hi, Mum!!' calls Juliet, putting on a really false smile.

'Where have you been?' says her dad.

'To see Larry,' says Juliet. 'We've been talking.' Then she looks down and says, 'Hey, Dad, I'm sorry I was so stroppy earlier on. I've thought about what you said and I can see sense now. I *will* marry Paris!'

'That's my girl!' roars Boss Capulet, putting his arm around her and giving her a kiss. 'Well, we won't waste any more time then! We'll have the wedding tomorrow! Cor! I'm well chuffed about this! I really am!'

'See, I told you she'd come round in the end!' says Ma Capulet giving them this real know-it-all look.

'Ange,' says Juliet. 'Will you help me do my nails and choose something to wear?'

'Course I will!' says Ange, and the two of them go upstairs.

Once they're in Juliet's bedroom, she and Ange look in her wardrobe. It's packed with dresses, tops, trousers, jackets and shoes. There must be hundreds of outfits in there. And most of them are the latest designer label stuff. I'm telling you, that Juliet was well spoilt!

Ange starts rummaging through the gear, grabbing outfits then holding them up against Juliet and saying things like, 'No, that won't do! Pink's so last season!' before chucking them on the floor and grabbing the next one. Then, just as she's making a start on Juliet's nails, Ma Capulet sticks her head round the door and says, 'You both OK? Need any help?'

'No thanks, Mum,' says Juliet. Then she does this big yawn and says, 'Listen, you two, I'm really tired and I want to be fresh for my big day. I need my beauty sleep. So, if it's OK with you, I'll go to bed now. I'm sure you've both got lots to do.'

'We certainly have, my dear!' says her mam. 'We must impress your new husband with our good taste and set an example to all the less-sophisticated people round here. After all, we are the poshest family on this estate. Come, Angela! We have cushions to plump and volley-vents to defrost. Goodnight, Juliet!'

'Sweet dreams!' says Ange, then they go downstairs.

Once she's sure they're gone, Juliet sits on her bed and opens the bottle of knock-out juice. But, just as she's going to drink it, she panics and wonders what she'll do if it doesn't work.

It isn't a problem! she thinks after a mo'. Then she takes a knife out of her bag and says, 'I really would cut my throat, rather than marry Paris!'

After that, she starts worrying about all sorts of other stuff. Like, what if Larry's tricking her? And what it'll feel like when she's lying next to all those stiffs at the undertaker's. But in the end she just says, 'Whatever!' lifts the bottle to her lips, whispers, 'Romeo, Romeo, Romeo! Here's drink – I drink to thee!' And swallows it all. A second later, she's out like a light!

Act Five
Nightmare!

Next morning, Boss Capulet is unpacking drinking glasses and paper plates, while Ange is filling little bowls with peanuts and Doritos and Ma Capulet is dashing about, spraying enough lavender-scented air freshener to kill a whole family of skunks.

'OK, Angela!' says Ma Capulet, all full of her own self-importance and putting on her most la-di-da voice. 'It's time for you to go and wake Juliet.'

'Yoo hoo, Jules! Wakey, wakey!' chirps Ange, bouncing into the bedroom. 'Come on, no lyin' in this mornin'! Today is your big day!'

But Juliet doesn't move. So Ange bends over and touches her cheek. It's freezing cold! And Juliet's not breathing! Two seconds later, Ange is downstairs with her face all white and quivery, and tears rolling down her cheeks.

'What is the matter, Angela?' says Ma Capulet, suddenly looking dead scared.

'She's... she's... DEAD!' screams Ange. 'Juliet is dead!'

'NO! NO! NO!' screams Ma Capulet, now completely forgetting her hoity-toity accent. 'You're wrong! She can't be! She can't be!' And they all go racing back up to the bedroom.

Boss Capulet checks for a pulse and now the Capulets know their daughter is dead (or so they think), they all begin moaning and cursing and screaming.

Which is when Larry walks in, along with Paris, who's all togged up in his best bling and Tommy Hilfiger, with about three litres of gel dripping off his spiked-up hair.

'Is she ready then?' says Paris, fiddling nervously with the massive gold chain that's dangling round his neck.

'Yeah, she's well ready, mate!' says Boss Capulet. 'Ready for her *funeral*!'

'What?' says Paris, his legs going all wobbly and his bottom lip starting to quiver. 'What do you mean "her funeral"? We're supposed to be getting married!'

'Not any more, you're not!' says Boss

Capulet. 'She's dead, mate. Ange found her all stiff and cold about ten minutes ago.'

And with that, they all start screaming and moaning again. Apart from Larry, who stays calm.

'Listen!' he says, suddenly pressing the palms of his hands together like he's about to start praying or something. 'You're all far too upset to think straight. Leave everything to me. I'll make sure Juliet's body gets taken to the Chapel of Rest. I'll sort out the arrangements for the funeral, too.'

Up in Manchester, Romeo's really looking forward to the time when he can be with Juliet. He's making himself nice and comfy, too, in the flat Larry's fixed him up with. But, of course, he's completely in the dark about Larry's new plan. Getting him up to speed on everything is now down to Larry's mate John getting to the flat, telling him what he's got to do and giving him the key to the funeral place.

But someone is about to beat John to it. And they're going to give Romeo the wrong story. Because they've no idea that Juliet isn't really dead. And that someone is... me! (Yeah, I know what you're thinking, just don't say it.)

Romeo's settling down to watch the footie, when there's a knock on the door. He switches off the TV, feeling a bit nervous now, thinking it might be a couple of Capulet lads come to do him in.

'Who is it?' he calls.

'It's me,' I say. 'Baz!'

So Romeo opens up.

'Baz, mate!' he says. 'You look well stressed! How's my gorgeous babe down in Nottingham then?'

'I got bad news, mate!' I say. Then, deciding there's no point in beating about the bush, I take a deep breath and say, 'Juliet's dead!'

'You're joking!' gasps Romeo. 'You gotta be!'

'No, mate, it's true,' I say. 'I heard it from Ange. So I caught the first National Express up here. I didn't want you to get the news from no one else.'

Romeo flops down on the sofa and puts his head in his hands. 'Dead?' he moans. 'No, not my Juliet. I just can't believe it.'

'It's true,' I say. 'Larry's already had her body taken up the funeral place. I'm really, really sorry, mate.'

At that instant Romeo makes a decision. But he doesn't tell me about it. He knows he can't live without Juliet, so he decides he'll just have to die with her. A moment later he gets out a notepad and scribbles a letter to his dad, telling him everything that's happened. And what he's planning to do. Then he says to me, 'Listen, Baz! We must get back to Nottingham. There's something I need to sort out.'

'All right, mate!' I say. 'But you got a really weird look on your face. You're not planning on doing something crazy, are you?'

'No, nothing like that,' says Romeo.

Two hours later, I'm waiting for Romeo outside a B&Q in Nottingham. And he's at the checkout, clutching a packet of rat poison.

Back at the youth club, John is also just back from Manchester.

'Hi, John!' says Larry. 'Did you get the message to Romeo?'

'Well, Larry,' says John, looking a bit uncomfortable. 'That's what I've come to see you about. Things didn't go as planned. When I was on my way to the flat, I bumped into an old mate. While we were chattin', I put down me bag an' some thief nicked it!'

'You're not safe anywhere nowadays, are you, John?' says Larry. 'Did the bag have much in it?'

'Everything!' says John. 'Romeo's address and phone number, my wallet, my dosh, my moby ... everything! I was stuck there and couldn't even use a payphone to tell you what's happened because of the cops and the Big E listening in on your calls.'

'Nightmare!' says Larry. 'So, Romeo's still no idea what's going on?'

'Not a clue!' says John. 'I'm real sorry, mate.'

'Hmm, this could be tricky,' says Larry. 'I reckon the best thing now is for me to go and get Juliet out of that funeral place. Then take her straight to Romeo in Manchester!'

'Good plan!' says John.

And it would have been, if only Larry had been a bit quicker off the mark.

Thing is, while he's been talking to John, Paris has been thinking about Juliet, too. He's really churning up inside and desperate to see her and say a few last words to her in private. So, that night he goes to the funeral place with this glass vase full of flowers.

He breaks the window, reaches in, opens it and climbs inside. It's dead dark in there, so he spends a few minutes trying to find Juliet's coffin. As soon as he's sure he's got the right one, he puts the flowers on it, blubbing all the time about how much he loved her and how he's so sorry she's dead. But then, all of a sudden, he hears footsteps outside.

Realising he's about to get company, Paris ducks down behind a cupboard. A few moments later, there's the sound of wood splintering. Then he sees the door opening really, really slowly and hears voices.

Of course, it's Romeo and me.

'Gimme that screwdriver, Baz!' says Romeo. Then he reaches in his pocket and takes out the letter he wrote in Manchester. 'Now listen, Baz!' he says, pointing his torch at Juliet's coffin. 'I wanna be alone right now, but would you do something for me? Give this letter to my dad, but not until tomorrow morning! Have you got that?'

'Sure,' I say. 'You know you can trust me.'

'An' listen!' says Romeo. 'Don't come sneaking back and spying on me. Cos if you do, I'll give you such a slapping you'll be eating hospital food for a month.'

'No probs, mate!' I say. 'I'm outta here!'

But, before I can leave, Romeo starts acting all weird. He takes hold of my hand and shakes it, saying, 'The best of luck for your future, mate! I hope you get everything you want in life.' Then he sticks his hand in his wallet, takes out a big wadge of tenners, and stuffs them in my top pocket.

Now obviously I didn't actually get to see all the gruesome stuff what went on next. But this is what the police worked out happened from what Larry told them and from all the evidence that was there.

The moment I'm gone, Romeo levers the lid off Juliet's coffin lid. Paris, who's still crouched behind the cupboard, is totally gobsmacked. Don't forget, Paris has no idea that Romeo's married to Juliet. Or even that he had a thing going with her. As far as he's concerned, Romeo's just the creep who murdered Tyrone (whose body also happens to be here), and this makes the whole situation even weirder.

83

He's sure Romeo's up to something. So he leaps out of his hiding place, grabs hold of him and says, 'Right! I've got you now, you murdering Montague! You know what the Big E said about coming back to Nottingham. You're a dead man!'

As it's so dark, Romeo can't see who's got hold of him, but he says, 'Yeah! I know I'm a dead man,' in this dreamy, couldn't-care-less sort of voice. 'That's why I came here. Look, mate, I'm feeling a bit stressed right now, so just lay off, will you? I don't wanna hurt you or anything. I just wanna be left in peace.'

But Paris doesn't listen! 'No way am I letting you go!' he yells, trying to drag Romeo towards the door. 'You're coming with me!'

'Leave it out, will you,' says Romeo, trying to shake Paris off.

But Paris just tightens his grip. So Romeo elbows him in the ribs. And next thing, they're rolling around the floor bashing into coffins. But it doesn't last long because Romeo, who's now gone completely nuts, grabs the nearest thing to him, which just happens to be Paris's glass vase. Then he smashes him over the head with it. As he does, Paris drops to his knees.

'You've done me!' he gasps, falling back on the floor. 'All I wanted was to see Juliet. Please lay me next to her. I really did love her.' And then he goes still.

Realising his attacker must be dead, Romeo shines his torch on him to get a better look. Which is when he finally sees who he's just killed. And he realises Paris was nuts about Juliet, too. So now he feels worse than ever.

'We're both sailing in the same unlucky boat!' he says sadly. 'Things just don't work out for some of us, do they?'

Then he picks up Paris's body, carries it to Juliet's coffin and lays it on the table next to her. He looks down at Juliet's beautiful, sleeping face and says, 'Well, love. At least I've got one thing to be thankful for. You may be dead, but you're still as gorgeous as ever. Which is more than I can say for Tyrone over there.' He lets out a really big sob. 'This has all turned out to be a right mess, my darling. I feel really bad about killing Tyrone, too, you know. But at least I'm going to punish his murderer.'

And with that, he climbs onto the table, swallows the rat poison and washes it down with a can of Coke. Two seconds later, he's dead.

Which is the exact moment Larry walks in. His torch immediately picks out Juliet's coffin. But then he spots the bodies lying either side of it and stops in his tracks. When he realises it's Romeo and Paris he's looking at, the shock is more than he can handle. He bends over and cries like a little kid.

But worse is to come! When Larry finally plucks up the courage to look in Juliet's coffin, he sees that she's waking up! He looks down at her, terrified, wishing he could make time stand still. But of course, it doesn't.

Juliet opens her eyes, smiles up at him and says, 'Oh, it's you, Larry.' She looks around, puzzled, but then she smiles again. 'Yes, I remember, I took that knock-out stuff, didn't I. So's I could be with my lovely Romeo again. And now I'm waking up in my coffin, just like you said I would. Thank you, Larry, thank you! But why do you look so unhappy? And where's Romeo? You promised me he'd be here when I woke up. I know he wouldn't let me down because he loves me more than anything in the world. Like I love him more than anything in the world.'

Larry can hardly bear to tell her. 'Listen, Juliet,' he says, as gently as he can. 'Things didn't go quite the way we planned. There was a bit of a mix-up and Romeo's...' But he can't say the word.

'And Romeo's what...?' says Juliet, looking like she's gonna scream at any moment. Then, before Larry can answer, she heaves herself out of the coffin and sees Romeo's body, with his lifeless eyes staring up at her. Her face crumples and she screams and begins tearing at her hair and clothes.

'Oh my poor, poor darling Romeo!' she yells. 'Life is too, too cruel! I never knew it could be this bad! I wish I'd never been born!'

'Listen, Juliet!' says Larry. 'I'm really, really sorry. But you don't want to hang around here. Come with me and I'll take you to some really kind people I know. They'll look after you.'

'I will not away!' screams Juliet. 'How can you think I would want to live after this?'

Things start happening really fast now. There are sirens and voices and footsteps outside the funeral place. Realising it's the cops, Larry knows he's got to get Juliet out of there, and fast.

But Juliet spots the empty packet in Romeo's hand and it hits her that he's poisoned himself. She falls on him and begins kissing his dead lips. As she does, her hand feels the knife in his pocket. She pulls it out. 'O happy dagger!' she says. 'This is thy sheath. There rust, and let me die!' And before Larry can stop her, she rams it deep into her chest. Then she does this big shudder and slumps on top of Romeo ... dead.

All at once, there's shouting and movement everywhere and the whole place is filled with people and this cop is pointing his torch at the bodies, saying, 'What the...!?'

There's more shouting and in rushes the Big E, followed by Ma Capulet and Boss Capulet and Boss Montague. The whole gruesome scene's completely lit up by the coppers' flashlights now. The sight of the three freshly killed, blood-soaked teenagers stops them in their tracks. All they can do is stare in disbelief at the bodies of their kids, and wonder if it's real. Or if they're having the worst nightmare of their lives. Then the cops bring in the body bags and they know it's true. They fall to their knees and moan and sob for their dead children.

I know what you're thinking. That the whole sorry mess was my fault. For dashing up to Manchester and telling Romeo that Juliet was dead, when she wasn't. But how was I to know? I just thought I was doing the right thing by my mate. Make no mistake though, I feel totally gutted about the whole thing. What I did is gonna stay with me for as long as I live. I just hope they're somewhere better now.

Looking on the positive side though, a bit of good *has* come out of it. First of all there was a big joint funeral for Romeo, Juliet, Paris and Tyrone, which everybody from the whole estate came to. I've never seen so many flowers in my life. Nor so many people blubbing and moaning at the same time. Including me. And just for once round our way, there was no scrapping. It was awesome!

Then, that evening after the funeral, Boss Capulet, Ma Capulet, the Big E and Boss Montague all sat down together in Mr Kwok's and decided there'd been enough aggro round here to last for some time. And they swore a sort of oath thingy, saying that they'd try and mend their ways and work to make the estate a better place to live, rather than forever trying to kill each other. And, finally, as a way of saying they were all really sorry for what had happened, they each chucked in a thousand quid to pay for one of them memorials. It's gonna be gold statues of Romeo and Juliet. And they're gonna be standing in the middle of the precinct, where this whole sorry story started.

I just hope they don't get vandalised.

About the Author

Michael Cox was born in Nottinghamshire and still lives there, with his wife and some fish. Michael loves reading, drawing, listening to music, eating, stretching and sleeping.

In the 1990s, Michael's story, 'Little Fred Riding Hood', won a Scholastic Independent Story of the Year award and since then he has written about 40 fiction and non-fiction books for children of all ages.

Michael first saw *Romeo and Juliet* performed at his secondary school when he was 12. Romeo was played by the head boy and Juliet was played by the head girl. Both of them had film-star looks and happened to be going out with each other, which obviously helped a lot in the romantic scenes. Michael says that during the final tragic death scene he was actually moved to tears. However, this could have been because the boy sitting next him had just punched him in the mouth.

When he first read Shakespeare in class, Michael was initially baffled by the language. But one day it all began to make sense and he realised how stunningly clever it was of Shakespeare to use words to say so much so briefly and so beautifully.

SHAKESPEARE TODAY

WILLIAM
SHAKESPEARE'S

A Midsummer Night's Dream

RETOLD BY
ROBERT
SWINDELLS

SHAKESPEARE TODAY

William Shakespeare's

AS YOU LIKE IT

Retold by Jenny Oldfield

Shakespeare Today

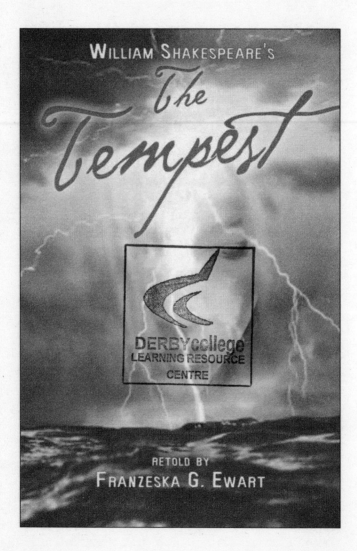

William Shakespeare's

The Tempest

RETOLD BY
Franzeska G. Ewart